MARIGOLD
and the Dark

Annie O'Dowd

NATIONAL
MARITIME
MUSEUM

When you see this harp
in the story, turn to Sea Gem's
Almanac of Strange Things on page 74.

1
Tea Time

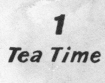

ARE YOU AFRAID OF THE DARK? I'm not. I don't know why, but to me the dark is like a soft cloak. I feel safe there, hidden from danger, veiled from the curious gaze of strangers. But there is someone I know who used to be absolutely terrified of the dark. Perhaps losing her parents at such a young age had made her that way. She was an orphan, you see, a foundling. Can you guess who I'm talking about? That's right, it's Marigold, Marigold Sandburrow.

Many months had passed since she had been rescued at sea. Left Shoe had found her floating in a basket, tossed in the waves of a wild storm. After that, his family had taken the little

baby seadog into their own burrow. Left Shoe's parents never found out what happened to Marigold's family, so they started to think of her as one of their very own pups. She had become Left Shoe's favourite, of course, and even though she wasn't his real twin, she was always at his side.

It wasn't long before the Sandburrow family noticed that Marigold was really frightened of the dark. The night-time made her uneasy, so she always slept with a lamp on. Its small halo of light pushed back the gloom and made her feel safe. Sometimes, though, the lamplight didn't help. She would wake in fright and howl into the blackness.

When Marigold tried to see in the dark she would stretch her eyes wide. But it didn't do any good; the shadows' smudgy edges took the forms of scary monsters and ghoulish ghosts. You see, this little pup had another problem. There was something wrong with her eyes. To Marigold, the world looked fuzzy. That's right; I knew you'd ask. Marigold was short-sighted and needed glasses. Old Cork and Blue Bottle hadn't noticed. They were too busy, as recently a new set of twins had been born. Babies, as you probably already know, are a lot of work.

Are you ready now for the story? In this amazing

adventure, Marigold finds herself alone with her worst fear. And what's more, she meets a creature that is the dread of seadogs, the horror of horrors … the goanna. This prehistoric lizard has extraordinary powers. For one thing, it has a very contagious laugh. If you ever hear that rattling sound, cover your ears! Otherwise you will laugh so hard you'll almost burst. I hope you won't be trembling with fright to hear this, but the ghastly, giggling goanna loves to eat seadogs, especially the tender seadog pup. To capture its prey, the goanna stares at it with shiny eyes. The poor victim is hypnotised in moments, and later, the goanna roasts it over the flames of a crackling fire.

On the night our story begins, Marigold was sitting next to the open window, sketching Left Shoe's long, brown face.

'Don't move, silly!' she protested.

'I'm trying not to. Hurry, Rig, I'm starving!'

Marigold smiled. She liked it when Left Shoe called her 'Rig'. It was his special name for her. She looked back at her drawing. It was hard to see it in the darkening room and she held the page closer to the lamp for better light. Her eyes still blurred. She stretched them wide and then tried to focus on her drawing.

'Are you all right, Rig?' Left Shoe asked.

'Fine,' said Marigold, and she held up her picture for him to admire.

The rest of the family were getting ready for dinner. Blue Bottle stood at the stove stirring seaweed mash with her youngest twin, Sea Gem, on her hip. Sea Gem was named for a piece of glass, smoothed by sand, roughened by the sea. Her eyes were the colour of the ocean and she was completely white. 🛡 As you know, seadogs are almost always brown, so at first this had worried her parents because she had to stay out of the hot sun. As she grew a little bigger, they noticed that Sea Gem was different in other ways, too. Her eyes often fixed on things that were invisible to everyone else. Also, her twin, Tumblegrass, already chattered away in complete sentences, but Sea Gem had never spoken a word.

Blue Bottle placed two bowls of mash on the table, and Old Cork lifted Sea Gem and Tumblegrass into their highchairs.

As the babies began eating happily, Blue Bottle turned to the older children.

'Left Shoe, would you set the table? Driftwood and Shark Tooth, please tidy up those toys. And Marigold, I need some

vinegar for the salad, could you fetch me some, please? If there isn't any in my work-snug, there's bound to be some in the dry-snug.'

Marigold turned to look at her mother, pale faced. She understood what that meant. There was always a lantern burning in Blue Bottle's work-snug. But the dry-snug was dark.

You might remember that a snug is a room in a seadog burrow. Some snugs are above ground and these are cheerful places with small, round windows. The dark snugs are gloomy caverns deeper underground and have no light apart from lantern or candle. Some are used as work-snugs, but others, even deeper in the earth, are musty storerooms. The dry-snug was one of these. It was piled with all kinds of foodstuffs: sacks of grass-seed flour, jams and fruit preserves, jars of oil and bottles of seaweed wine. But worst of all, directly underneath the dry-snug was the scariest snug in the whole burrow, the worm-snug.

Marigold attempted a frozen-looking smile to pretend that she wasn't frightened.

'Take the lantern,' encouraged Blue Bottle. 'You'll be fine.'

'All right,' Marigold said slowly, and she looked around the room to see if anyone might come with her. But Shark Tooth and Driftwood were piling toys into a basket and Left Shoe was busy with paws full of spoons. Poor Marigold knew that she would just have to be brave.

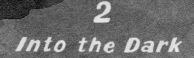

2
Into the Dark

MARIGOLD CLUTCHED THE LANTERN tightly in her paw and walked purposefully along the shadowy tunnel. Just ahead she could see the welcome glow of light coming from Blue Bottle's work-snug. With relief, she scampered through its open doorway and, once inside, scanned the shelves that lined the walls. She held her lantern close to the neat rows of bottles to read their labels. The wiggly lines blurred. She had only just started to learn her letters, but she knew that vinegar started with a 'v', and that its bottle was a tall, green one.

'V is for vinegar,' she said quietly to herself as she carefully checked each bottle. Her heart sank. There was definitely no vinegar. She would have to go down into the dark dry-snug.

As you can imagine, this idea was a very unhappy one for Marigold. But she needed to find the vinegar, so she went to the centre of the snug, where there was a rickety trapdoor on the floor. She placed her lantern next to the entrance and opened the rusty latch. With a shiver, she climbed into the black opening and then retrieved her light. As she stepped carefully down the ladder into the cool, dark space, the lantern swung spookily, casting spiky shadows. In the gloom, she could see sacks of grass-seed flour, crates of fruit, and brown earthenware pots of honey. It smelled of grain and apples. It was so quiet that the only sound was the little in and out 'whoosh' of her breath, and the occasional squeak of the lantern.

Marigold's heart started to pound. She was thinking again of the worm-snug, directly beneath her. The worm-snug was the blackest place you could imagine. It was as dark as the grave, as sunless as midnight on the bottom of the sea. Even worse, it lay next to the roots of a large casuarina tree. Like spidery veins, the tangled mass pushed its way through the walls. Amongst those dark tendrils, worms wriggled; spiders scuttled.

Marigold descended the last rungs of the dry-snug's ladder and then held the lantern high. There it was – the vinegar! Though a little blurry, she recognised the bottles stacked on a low shelf next to a sack of apples. Marigold felt overcome with relief. She squinted in the dimness, trying to work out what was making the black shadow in the middle of the snug. She couldn't see it properly. Deciding that it was just an ordinary shadow, Marigold bravely scampered towards the vinegar. Too late, she realised that the shadow was the open doorway of the worm-snug. The hapless pup stepped right into its round opening and fell down into the darkness with a terrified bark. She dropped the lantern and the light went out.

Marigold lay in dank blindness. For a moment, she wasn't sure what had happened. Thankfully she was unhurt as the floor of the worm-snug was of soft earth. It was damp as well. Her arm rested in a small puddle, which smelled of mud and rotting leaves. The dark enveloped her, as thick as winter quilts. She whispered, 'V is for vinegar,' to make sure she was still alive. Her tiny voice sounded hollow in that total dark. Marigold was very, very frightened. She was sure that ghosts and spiders or snakes and goannas lay hiding in that blanket of blackness. She felt a soft tap on her forehead. Something had fallen on her and, with a shudder, she brushed it away with her paw. Then another small plop followed, except this time it fell on her nose and slithered wetly. It was a worm! Its sliminess was so terrifying that she howled in distress. Then, a light appeared above her.

'ARE YOU DOWN THERE, MARIGOLD?' shouted a voice from above. The lantern descended the ladder and Marigold could just make out the flash of Old Cork's glasses in its glow.

'Marigold! I heard your howl,' he barked. 'Are you all right?'

Marigold managed to sit up and nod her head mutely. Old Cork knelt at her side and stroked her ears.

'Are you hurt?' he asked anxiously.

Marigold shook her head. 'I fell in,' she said in a small voice.

The worm-snug had once been used as a storeroom. But in the lantern's light they could see it was now a jumble of empty boxes draped in cobwebs, stacks of timber and piles of old junk. Next to where Marigold sat was a crumbling patch of wall, where a dark mass of tangled, knotted tree roots snaked through the mouldering plaster. Clinging to these roots in hideous, writhing clumps were thousands of worms. They dropped to the floor and slithered through the ceiling. Old Cork held the lantern high for a closer look.

'Father,' whimpered Marigold, 'I don't like the dark.'

'Hush now,' Old Cork soothed. He picked her up and Marigold clung to him, trembling. 'You know that the dark is only dark because there isn't any light,' he said. 'See?' Old Cork put the lantern behind his back so their faces were obscured in the dimness. 'Now watch,' continued her father, 'I'm going to chase the dark away.' He held the lantern up and the darkness receded.

Marigold managed a watery smile, but she wasn't convinced. Old Cork was only saying that to make her feel better.

'The vinegar is in the dry-snug,' said Marigold in a quavery voice. 'Can we go now?'

'All right then, we'll fetch it on our way back. Hmmm,' growled Old Cork, having a final look around. 'It's a terrible mess down here.'

When they reached the cooking-snug, the babies had finished their mash and were splashing in a tin tub next to the stove. Blue Bottle added the vinegar to the salad and placed it on the table. The rest of the family took their places and began to eat hungrily. Marigold only had a few mouthfuls, and then stared gloomily at the bottles sitting in a row on the bench. They were the medicines her mother had been making that day to sell at the market, carefully labelled in Blue Bottle's scribbly handwriting. Marigold squinted to see if she could read any of the letters on the labels, but the squiggly lines blurred.

'Are you all right, Marigold?' asked Old Cork.

'I have a headache … My eyes feel funny.'

'Hmmm,' said Old Cork. He looked at her strangely and thought for a moment. Then he suddenly spoke. 'Marigold, can you see the numbers on the clock over there?' Marigold listlessly lifted one ear, then let it flop down again. She shook her head.

Old Cork and Blue Bottle looked at each other meaningfully, and then took turns asking her some more questions. Whose coat was hanging on the hook? What was leaning against the door? Could she read the date on the calendar?

Marigold shook her head. There was a moment of silence.

Suddenly Old Cork clapped his paws. 'I'm afraid you need glasses, my girl,' he said jovially. 'I'll make them for you myself.'

Marigold was quiet. She blinked back tears and looked down at her lap. She didn't want to wear glasses. Glasses would look strange on her. She knew that Left Shoe was always misplacing his. Only last week he'd broken them and had had to wait for a whole day while they were repaired. Added to this, he couldn't wear them swimming, and when he was sailing he had to be careful not to drop them into the water.

'Don't worry,' Old Cork added in a softer tone, 'you'll see much better if you wear them.'

Marigold didn't speak. Tears gathered in her eyes again and further blurred her despairing gaze.

4
Market Day

MARIGOLD WOKE THE NEXT MORNING feeling happy. Sunlight slanted though the crack in her curtains. She sat up in bed, pulled back the drapes and opened the window. A cool breeze ruffled the surface of the sea, and small puffs of white cloud made their way across the sky. Saturday! Market day! She could see blurry boats far out on the horizon and she imagined the many different goods that they might carry: hardware or grain, rolls of cloth, food or second-hand goods. All were headed to the market, which was held a short distance from Foamy Bay village. Marigold was wishing that she was going too when a cool gust of wind came

16

through the window, making her shiver. She shut the window and jumped out of bed.

As she rummaged through her drawers for her favourite dress, the events of the night before suddenly came back to her. Old Cork had said she would need to wear glasses. Marigold walked over to the mirror  and studied her reflection. She tried to imagine how she would look wearing glasses. Marigold frowned. She didn't want glasses! Sighing with vexation, she searched her floor and under the bed for her dress. Finally she spied it neatly folded on top of the chest of drawers. Quickly pulling it on, Marigold scampered into the cooking-snug for breakfast.

Left Shoe was already eating seed cakes and sipping a large cup of squink. Old Cork was standing at the stove toasting rows of seed cakes while Sea Gem sat in her highchair, chewing on a crust.

Marigold took her place next to Left Shoe. Blue Bottle put some hot seed cakes in front of her, and then poured herself a cup of squink and sat down.

'Your father and I have been talking about your glasses, Marigold,' Blue Bottle said. 'Old Cork wants to start making

17

them straight away, but he needs some wire for the frames.' She began turning her cup in her paws. 'I'm very busy this morning, so I thought that maybe you two would like to go to market to buy some.'

'You mean, just Marigold and me … by ourselves?' asked Left Shoe.

'Yes,' replied Blue Bottle with a smile. 'It would be a big help to your father and me.'

'Hooray!' cried Marigold, laughing in delight.

'While you finish your breakfast,' continued Blue Bottle, 'I'll show you what I'd like you to take.' Blue Bottle had made a neat stack of jars, packets and bottles on the bench. She wrote down a list of how many cuttlebones  they should ask for each. Blue Bottle handed Left Shoe the list. On the back she had written down all the things that she wanted the children to buy. Left Shoe read it out to Marigold.

2 bottles of banksia wine – 1 cuttlebone
1 roll of thin wire – 2 cuttlebones
newspaper (*Weekly Bark*) – ½ cuttlebone
1 bottle of pink fig cordial – ½ cuttlebone
1 box of icing sugar – ½ cuttlebone
1 packet of birthday candles – 2 cuttlebones

'Who are the birthday candles for?' asked Marigold, when she heard the last item.

Blue Bottle and Old Cork glanced at each other and then turned to Marigold.

'It's Left Shoe's birthday next week,' said Blue Bottle.

Marigold looked at her brother happily. He was folding the list and putting it into his pocket. She was going to ask when her birthday was, but then remembered that no one really knew.

Old Cork and Blue Bottle carefully packed the wares and the children's morning tea and lunch into their satchels, and Old Cork gave Left Shoe some extra cuttlebones to buy sweets. When they were ready to go, Blue Bottle turned to face the pair.

'Now remember, stay close together at the market. Marigold, you hold Left Shoe's paw, won't you? And watch out for

snakes, and especially goannas.' Marigold and Left Shoe had never actually seen a goanna, but had been warned about them for as long as they could remember. They nodded solemnly to assure their parents that they would be careful.

Blue Bottle smiled. She kissed Marigold and went to do the same for Left Shoe, but he ducked and hurried out the door.

'Bye, Mother,' he said, laughing.

'Remember, watch out for goannas,' she called after them.

Sea Gem climbed down from her highchair and followed the children through the doorway. Running after them, she began to howl.

'Whatever is the matter, Sea Gem?' asked Blue Bottle, following her.

'Perhaps she wants to go too,' said Old Cork with a chuckle.

Blue Bottle picked up the baby seadog, and Sea Gem pointed her paw towards the beach. She fixed her pale eyes on Left Shoe and Marigold until they were out of sight.

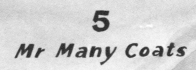

5
Mr Many Coats

MARIGOLD AND LEFT SHOE walked along the sea's edge. Now and again, they jumped over the waves or ran up the beach to avoid a splashing. They had long passed the last burrows of their village and the sun was rising higher in the sky.

'Let's have some morning tea,' Left Shoe suggested. They turned towards the line of bush beyond the beach and settled themselves in the dappled shade of a fig tree. They ate in silence, looking over the sea, and when they'd finished, Marigold pulled paper and coloured pencils from her satchel. While she sketched the blue sweep of ocean, Left Shoe repacked the bags.

'Come on, Rig, we'd better get going.'

'All right, just let me finish this,' Marigold replied, adding some passing boats to her picture.

'Well, hurry up then, because we have to find the market short cut and it's nearly lunchtime already.' Left Shoe waited a few moments, standing next to the bags. Marigold was squinting at some white sea birds that had flown into view. She tried to add their blurred forms to her picture.

'Marigold! Come on,' said Left Shoe impatiently.

'Nearly finished,' she replied, her gaze returning to the birds.

Her brother sighed and looked towards their destination. 'The short cut must be nearby,' he said suddenly. 'I'll just go and see if I can find it. You wait right here.'

Marigold nodded distractedly and, after a moment's hesitation, Left Shoe scampered into the undergrowth.

Only a few minutes later, a long shadow darkened Marigold's page. At first she paid no attention to it, thinking a cloud had passed in front of the sun. But then a voice said, 'Good morning, Miss.'

Marigold looked up in surprise. Towering over her was a very tall gentleman. He certainly wasn't a seadog. She couldn't see him very well because he was all blurry and the sun was behind him, but she could tell that the creature was entirely green, with leathery-looking skin. He moved closer, and his shiny black eyes came into focus. They glinted as he lowered his head to Marigold.

'Are you well?' asked the gentleman politely.

'Yes …' said Marigold. She wasn't sure what to say to him, and looked around to see if Left Shoe was returning yet.

'It's a beautiful morning,' said the creature. His voice sounded like rustling dry leaves.

Marigold regarded him with some curiosity. The fellow seemed to be dressed in a variety of coats, one on top of the other. The topmost coat was of lovely purple velvet.

'Aren't you hot?' she asked boldly. The creature said nothing, but looked at her, smiling. His eyes were so shiny. They were like wet pebbles, or precious jewels, as ink black as the worm-

snug. Marigold felt that she could gaze into them forever. They were so glassy; she could see her fuzzy reflection in their strange spheres. She had a soft, drowsy feeling, as if she were floating above herself. Then she dropped to the ground, fast asleep.

Meanwhile, Left Shoe had found the market track and returned, running to the beach. He saw his sister lying at the feet of a very strange creature.

'Marigold!' he barked. She did not reply but slept on, making little snoring sounds.

Left Shoe looked at the tall, leathery gentleman standing over her. He had never seen a lizard as large, nor one wearing such odd clothing.

'Good morning,' said the creature, flicking his tail. 'Is this your twin?'

'Yes,' said Left Shoe distractedly. 'Well, she's not my real twin, she's a foundling.'

'Ah, a foundling,' said the creature, and a red, forked tongue showed through his lipless mouth. 'Forgive me for not introducing myself,' he said with a polite bow. 'Mr Many Coats, at your service.'

Marigold made a soft growling sound.

'Marigold!' Left Shoe cried. 'Wake up!' His thoughts quickened in fear as he watched the green fellow out of the corner of his eye. Was he a goanna? Left Shoe thought about the characteristics of goannas: green, leathery skin that hangs loosely; yes, he had that. Black, beady eyes and a red, forked tongue; yes, those too. Evil, despicable nature? He wasn't really sure, as the strange fellow seemed kind as he leaned over Marigold.

Left Shoe shook Marigold gently. 'Come on, Rig, wake up!'

But she did not wake. Left Shoe wasn't sure what to do. He began to panic. 'We have to go to market, and we have to –'

'Calm yourself, young man,' interrupted Mr Many Coats. 'She probably just has a touch of sunstroke. Why don't we carry your sister to my camp? It's nearby. I could make you a cup of cordial.' Mr Many Coats smiled his toothless smile. 'And before you worry yourself, I'm not a goanna. So fret no more, my friend! I am a lizard, which is similar, but not at all dangerous to seadogs. There are plenty of us around these parts.'

Left Shoe was relieved to hear this. 'All right then,' he replied slowly, picking up the bags, 'but only until Marigold wakes up. We have to get going to the market.' The lizard tenderly picked up the sleeping pup, and Left Shoe followed him into the dense bracken.

Presently, they arrived at a clearing. The creature directed them into a small, one-roomed house made in a hollow tree.

They went inside and Marigold was set on a soft cushion next to the window.

'There, there, little one,' said Mr Many Coats, clicking his shivery, forked tongue. He patted Marigold with one of his clawed hands.

Looking around the small room, Left Shoe saw that there were only a few pieces of furniture, but they were tidily arranged. A rusty jam tin holding a bunch of bright red bottlebrush flowers brightened the small table, and next to the window there was a little stove. On the surface a saucepan bubbled. Grey foam spilled over the edges and it smelled unpleasantly of dead jellyfish.

'I've heard that lizards can be dangerous,' Left Shoe said suddenly. The creature paused, as still as a statue. Then a strange thing happened. The weird reptile began to chuckle, then giggle, then laugh. He laughed and laughed. You can try to imagine the sound of such a laugh, but until you actually hear it, you'll never understand. It sounded like a shower of stones, like seeds shaking in seedpods. It was a very contagious kind of laugh, which means that when you hear it, you can't help laughing yourself. Left Shoe held his sides and began to laugh too.

'Dear, silly boy!' said the creature, suddenly collecting himself. Left Shoe stopped laughing as well, and a tiny thought began to take shape in the back of his mind.

'Stop looking so worried,' said Mr Many Coats. 'We lizards aren't interested in seadog dinners. Now, how about that cordial?' He opened the little door in the cupboard behind him and retrieved the bottle of green cordial and two tin cups.

'We only eat beetles and worms – and frogs, of course,' he added casually, flicking his tongue in and out while he poured the drinks. He replaced the bottle tidily.

Left Shoe took a sip of the strange-smelling liquid.

'Do you like my spider cordial?'

Left Shoe choked, and only managed to swallow the bitter mouthful with great effort.

'Never mind, my young friend,' the lizard said, 'I have a plan. You said that you were going to market. Why don't you leave the sleeping foundling here, and I'll look after her until you get back?'

Left Shoe thought for a moment. He glanced at Marigold, snoring peacefully, and then back again to the strange fellow.

'Thank you, but I promised my parents that I would look after Marigold. I'll stay with her until she wakes up, if you don't mind.'

'Well, all right,' Mr Many Coats replied. He

regarded Left Shoe intently with his oily black eyes.

Left Shoe began to gaze into their inky spheres without knowing why. His mind felt feather-light, as if he were on a soft cloud. He was sleepy, but he wanted to keep staring into the glistening eyes, as shiny as wet stones. It was then that he remembered the little thought that had been growing in his mind. It had turned into a much bigger thought now. It was the laugh.

What was it that Blue Bottle had always told him? He couldn't quite remember. He felt dreamy, as if he were looking down at himself from a great height. Mr Many Coats spoke. His voice came from far away.

'Leave the foundling here, my young friend. Pick up your bags, go to market, and I'll see you when you return.'

This seemed suddenly like a very sensible idea. 'All right then,' said Left Shoe. His voice felt like it belonged to someone else. Shouldering the satchels, he walked calmly through the door of the hollow tree house, leaving Marigold asleep on the cushion. As he headed out of the clearing, he didn't notice the scatter of bones around the blackened remains of a campfire.

6
At the Market

LEFT SHOE WALKED THE REST of the way to the market. His mind was empty. It was as if he was in a strange dream. When he tried to make sense of it, no thoughts came. He reached the tents and colourful flags of the market, threw down the satchels and rested for a moment.

'Hello, Left Shoe.'

He looked up to see his cousins, Brass Button and Pink Shell, standing beside him. Pink Shell held a balloon on a long string and Brass Button munched on a cake with icing.

'Are you all right, Left Shoe?' Brass Button asked, looking at him closely.

'Fine,' he replied dreamily.

'What are you doing here?' asked Pink Shell.

'I'm selling Mother's medicines and honey, and I have to buy some things, too,' said Left Shoe.

'Where's Marigold?' asked Brass Button, finishing off his cake and licking some icing off his paw.

'She's sick,' replied Left Shoe. At least, he thought she was, but he couldn't quite remember.

'Poor Marigold,' said Pink Shell.

They were quiet for a moment, and then Brass Button picked up one of Left Shoe's bags. 'Come on, we'll help you do your shopping and then we can all walk home together, can't we, Pink?'

'All right,' said Left Shoe, standing up and lifting the other satchel over one shoulder.

As they entered the busy market, there was a little band playing a happy marching tune, and jugglers doing tricks with coloured balls. Left Shoe again had an uncomfortable feeling that something was not right, but he kept being distracted by the bustle. Some stalls were housed in striped tents; others stood in the open air and were marked with painted signs. One read 'Flour and Grain' and next to it another advertised 'Pots and Pans'.

'What do you have to do?' asked Brass Button. Left Shoe handed him the folded list from his pocket.

'All right,' said Brass Button, pacing up and down in an

important way. He read the list and then divided Blue Bottle's wares between them. With the cuttlebones they received, each agreed to shop for a couple of items on the list.

'Now, let's go and see who can be back first!' said Brass Button. 'We can meet over there, under that tree.' He pointed to a quiet spot where a little, brightly coloured tent stood. The sign on the front read 'Fortune Teller'.

They all agreed and the young seadogs quickly dispersed, each on their separate errands.

Meanwhile, back at the burrow, Sea Gem sat on a rug on the kitchen floor with her toys. Blue Bottle lifted a tray of golden cupcakes from the oven, and turned them out on a rack to cool. The peace was disturbed when Old Cork raced through the door in a frenzy of activity. He had already been through twice that morning, once covered in mud and carrying a tall tower of boxes, and the second time with a shovel and pick. Each time he'd shared a conspiratorial wink with Blue Bottle. Now he carried a pile of junk outside and returned with buckets and brushes. On his way past, he sampled one of the little cakes from the rack.

'Old Cork,' Blue Bottle scolded, 'they're for the party!'

Old Cork smiled sheepishly, and scurried off in the direction of his work-snug.

Sea Gem was humming and staring out of the window when all of a sudden, she pointed her ears upwards. They quivered and her blue eyes darkened. Her whole body trembled. She lifted her nose in the air and howled.

'Oh no! What happened?' exclaimed Blue Bottle. She looked around, but nothing was out of place. Blue Bottle picked her up. She had never heard Sea Gem cry so pitifully. She tried to quiet her but it was no use; Sea Gem howled and howled. Finally, Blue Bottle carried her down into the dry-snug, because dark places always soothed Sea Gem. From there they could hear muffled bangs and crashes coming from Old Cork's work-snug.

After a few moments, Sea Gem's sad wails quietened but she still quivered with anxiety. Then, in that soft darkness, she said her first word. 'Marigold!'

'Sea Gem!' gasped Blue Bottle with a smile, 'WHAT did you say?'

'Marigold,' Sea Gem said again, and her pale eyes hovered in the gloom, fierce with urgency.

After Left Shoe had finished his jobs, he went off in the direction of the meeting place. As he walked, a dark feeling

niggled at him. Something was definitely not right, but he couldn't think what it was. Anxiety quickened his pace and, weaving his way through the crowd, he arrived at the fortune teller's tent. Pink Shell and Brass Button had not yet returned, so he waited beside the entrance. He hadn't been standing there long when a voice from within the tent wafted through the doorway.

'Cross my paw with a cuttlebone and I'll tell you your future.'

Left Shoe peered into the tent. Sitting behind a round table, draped in scarves and exotic shell necklaces, was a seer.  She was entirely white, like Sea Gem.

'Come in,' she invited. Her voice was whispery, a thin swishy sound like waves on sand, and her eyes looked as if she were staring out to sea.

'Let me look into your future, young man ...' said the strange lady. She turned her opaque eyes towards him. Left Shoe, fascinated, stepped into the tent and sat down on the little chair in front of her.

The fortune teller took Left Shoe's paw, and her eyes widened. 'Something is wrong. You have been hypnotised!' From a pocket in her apron, she retrieved a small, stoppered bottle. She uncorked it and waved it under Left Shoe's nose.

A sharp smell emanated from it and Left Shoe's mind instantly cleared. The dreamy feeling disappeared, but still he could not recall why he felt uneasy. He watched the fortune teller thoughtfully as she pulled a piece of patterned silk from the table, revealing a crystal ball.

'Now that you're feeling better,' she said in her soft voice, 'let me tell your fortune ♥ – only one cuttlebone.'

Marigold stirred in her sleep and then rolled over. Her paw knocked against something hard and she shifted again to try to get more comfortable. Then, sleepily opening her eyes, she sat up. It wasn't daytime anymore, it was pitch black. Marigold felt a prickle of fear. Had she been asleep for that long? The last thing she could remember was the nice leathery gentleman looking into her eyes. Now she wasn't on the beach any more, but somewhere else entirely. There was a dreadful stench in that airless place. It was a disgusting smell, a smell of something so rotten and foul that she felt sick to her stomach. With trembling paws, she reached outwards into the blackness. She touched smooth wood. It was all around her, except for one part, which felt like an iron door. She explored it with her paws but couldn't open it. Marigold's heart hammered wildly as panic overcame her. What terrible place was this? Where was Left Shoe? Marigold curled into a ball and wept. She was trapped, a prisoner in the dark!

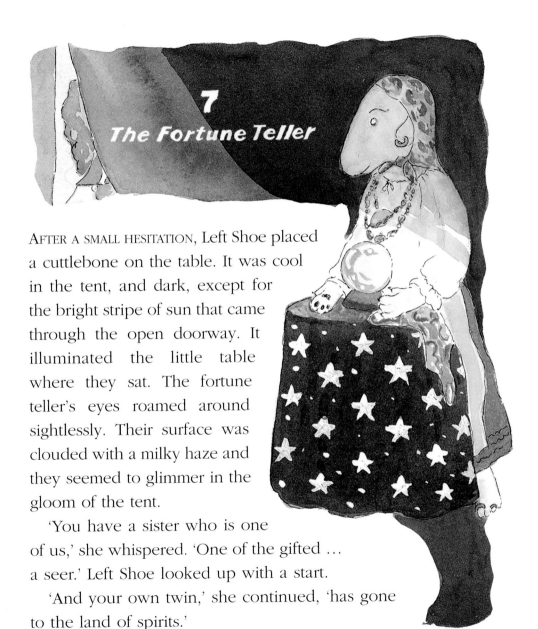

7
The Fortune Teller

AFTER A SMALL HESITATION, Left Shoe placed
a cuttlebone on the table. It was cool
in the tent, and dark, except for
the bright stripe of sun that came
through the open doorway. It
illuminated the little table
where they sat. The fortune
teller's eyes roamed around
sightlessly. Their surface was
clouded with a milky haze and
they seemed to glimmer in the
gloom of the tent.

'You have a sister who is one
of us,' she whispered. 'One of the gifted …
a seer.' Left Shoe looked up with a start.

'And your own twin,' she continued, 'has gone
to the land of spirits.'

How could this stranger know that? Left Shoe thought.

The white lady began to sway gently and sing a song under her breath. Its sad melody had a beautiful sound – sweet, silvery and soft. Left Shoe listened, and the warm notes seemed to sing inside him as well.

The seer closed her eyes and then opened them sharply.

'You have defeated a giant squid and rescued a pup at sea. One day you will save your village for a second time. Look into my crystal ball now, be my eyes.'

Left Shoe, astonished by what she'd said, gazed into the starry depths of the glassy ball. There were tiny lights that began to move and shimmer, and then swirl. Gradually, a hazy picture appeared. When I say a picture, it wasn't exactly how you might see something in the everyday world. In fact, it was almost as if Left Shoe was in the picture too. He was in his little boat, bracing himself against pounding waves. A strong smell of the sea overcame him. The crash of wild waves filled the little dark tent. Then he saw Marigold, a tiny baby in her basket, skimming down a gigantic wave. The seer spoke.

'She is called Marigold … the foundling.'

Left Shoe gasped as he remembered that Marigold had set out with him that morning to the market. Where was she? He tried to recall what had happened, but it was as if a dark curtain in his mind hid the answer.

When Marigold had worn herself out with weeping, she sat up and leant against the cool, dark wall. She tried to work out what had happened. Another wave of panic assailed her. It seemed to Marigold that the dark had swallowed her up, that she was invisible. She took very deep breaths to try to calm down. After a few moments, her heartbeat slowed. She tried to think about things slowly and clearly. Marigold decided that it must have something to do with that lizard gentleman. He must have locked her in here!

Then she heard a very weird noise coming from somewhere outside. It was an extraordinary sound, a clicking, whirring chuckle, like a shower of stones or a spray of sticks in the wind. It gave Marigold the strangest feeling. She wanted to laugh. Suddenly she found it horribly funny that she was imprisoned in the blackest dungeon that you can imagine. She laughed out loud. The sound of her giggle in all that dark made her feel better. She laughed again, and the more she laughed, the funnier it seemed. She laughed so hard that she gasped for breath. It started to hurt her and she clutched her sides in desperate mirth.

As Left Shoe gazed into the crystal ball, the tiny lights began to wink and then swirl again.

'Look ... the foundling,' the fortune teller whispered.

Then Left Shoe smelled something rotten, something decaying and foul. The picture in the ball swam into view. It was a leathery lizard dressed in an array of coats. The topmost one was ragged and soiled with rust-coloured stains. For a moment Left Shoe thought that he looked familiar. The creature was laying wood for a fire. More lizards came into view. They laughed silently. The picture faded as another took shape. It was a large tree fitted with an iron door. Then Left Shoe saw Marigold – she was locked inside it, in the dark! He breathed in sharply. The air around him filled with the sound of weeping. Or was it laughing? The thought that had been bothering Left Shoe for most of the day suddenly returned to his mind. It was the laugh of the goanna that his mother had warned him about! As this thought took shape, the rest of Left Shoe's memory returned.

At that same moment the seer grabbed Left Shoe's paw and, with terrible irony, Left Shoe already knew what she was going to say. 'It's Marigold ... she has been captured by goannas!'

BRASS BUTTON AND PINK SHELL were sitting under the tree next to the fortune teller's tent, waiting for Left Shoe. They were sampling bags of sweets they'd bought at the sweet stall, when they noticed someone rushing out of the tent. It was Left Shoe! He paused in the doorway, speaking to a seadog inside, and then appeared to put something in his satchel.

'Over here, Left Shoe,' Pink Shell called. But there was no need. Left Shoe had already seen them and was running in their direction.

'Marigold's in danger!' cried Left Shoe. 'I haven't got time to explain. We've got to hurry.'

The cousins scampered towards the market track. Left Shoe led the way, dodging between carts loaded with goods and busy seadogs coming and going. They had no time to lose. Left Shoe's heart quickened in anxiety. He hoped that they would not be too late.

When they arrived at the goannas' camp, there was no one about. In the centre of the clearing a campfire crackled, sending a smudge of smoke into the darkening afternoon. The three pups crouched behind a nearby bush as Left Shoe explained breathlessly what had happened on the way to the market, and what he had seen in the fortune teller's crystal ball. The cousins gaped in horror.

'Do you mean to tell us that you were both hypnotised, and now Marigold is imprisoned by goannas?' barked Brass Button.

'Yes, that's exactly what I mean,' replied Left Shoe. From his satchel, he pulled out a small, purple drawstring bag that the fortune teller had given him. Inside were a pair of dark glasses and three sets of cloth earplugs. He explained to his cousins how they could protect themselves from the goannas' laugh, and Brass Button and Pink Shell listened, pale faced.

'Great squirting molluscs!' said Brass Button in a strangled whisper. 'Are you sure this will work?'

'It just has to,' Left Shoe replied.

At that moment, rattling voices announced the arrival of four goannas into the clearing. Brass Button gasped loudly as two

of the dreadful lizards set up a metal frame across the fire. 'Oh no, the terrible roasting spit!' he squeaked.

Presently, the goannas took seats on the surrounding logs, talking all the while in their strange, rustling voices. Left Shoe recognised Mr Many Coats, even though he had exchanged his fine velvet coat for one that was ragged, stained and filthy.

'She's such a tender pup – I can't wait to chew her chops!' said the first goanna. He looked very old; his back was hunched and he wore a pair of glasses on the end of his wrinkled nose. Left Shoe saw Mr Many Coats take some tin cups and a bottle from behind a log. He then began to pour some disgusting-looking, lime-coloured drink into the cups.

'Yes, she'll be a tasty morsel,' mused Mr Many Coats. 'I put her in the dungeon.' He gestured to the tree fitted with the iron door that Left Shoe had seen in the crystal ball.

'Of course, her brother will be back soon,' continued Mr Many Coats, 'and then we can cook him as well.' He took a sip from his cup, and licked his lips with his shivery tongue. 'Then again, his flesh might be a little tough. He's a bit old for my tastes.'

'Oh, I don't know,' replied an evil-eyed lady goanna who wore a grimy-looking dress. 'Any seadog will do!' Then, horribly, the goannas began to chuckle.

'Quick,' said Left Shoe, gesturing that they should use the earplugs. The three friends stopped their ears and looked from one to the other. They knew they were all in great danger, very great danger indeed.

Marigold had felt so exhausted from laughing that she had fallen asleep for a while. When she awoke, it took her a moment to remember where she was. Strangely, she wasn't so frightened any more. All that giggling had made her feel better. But all the same she knew she would rather not laugh as long and as hard ever again. Then she remembered what Blue Bottle had always told her about the goanna laugh. Of course! Those weren't harmless lizards out there, they were goannas! She realised that she hadn't seen the lizard gentleman very clearly on the beach. She hadn't seen what he really was. Maybe she did need glasses after all. But for now, her eyesight was the least of her problems. She had to do something quickly, before the goannas laughed again. Marigold felt around the floor of the dungeon. It was empty except for dry grass and dead leaves. These she scrunched into some very scratchy wads and put them in her ears.

Outside, just beyond the clearing, the cousins removed their earplugs to discuss their plight in earnest whispers. Brass Button clutched his sister's paw. He cleared his throat and swallowed nervously.

'What can we do, Left Shoe?'

Left Shoe didn't answer directly, but gathered his cousins into a huddle and explained his plan.

'But that's too dangerous!' protested Pink Shell.

'No,' he replied, 'I got Marigold into this mess and I'm going to get her out of it. I'm going to trick Mr Many Coats like he tricked me!'

As Marigold sat in that stuffy, dark place, she started to feel worried again. Then she remembered what Old Cork had told her in the worm-snug. She tried to imagine her father's lantern as he held it up, pushing away the gloom. She took a deep breath and focused her mind by looking into the dark. Its inky blackness surrounded her like a heavy cloak. She fixed her eyes on it, watching the dark, seeing what the dark would do. Several minutes passed and still she stared, waiting. After a while she felt much calmer. It was then that something occurred to her. She realised that Old Cork was right. The dark wasn't absolutely real. Your hand passes through it, doesn't it? Marigold knew something else, too. If she had a candle right now, the dark would disappear, wouldn't it? If she had her father's lantern, the black would vanish in its pale halo of light. When Marigold considered the darkness that way, it didn't seem as frightening. In fact now, after staring at it for so long, it wasn't so very pitch black after all. Not completely coal black. Not as totally dark as the awful worm-snug. She noticed the pale shape of her dress in the dimness, and when she looked up, she could see a tiny pinprick of light.

Marigold stood up and looked towards it. Gathering her courage, she formed a plan in her mind. At last, with brave resolve, she fastened her claws onto the wooden walls. She began climb upwards towards the tiny light. Marigold's fear seemed to diminish as she climbed higher and, when she reached the small, winking light, she poked it with her paw. To her amazement, she found that the ceiling crumbled at her touch and showered her with dirt and twigs. She coughed in the choking scatter of debris. When she recovered, she looked up and saw a circle of sky!

9
Feeble Jokes

LEFT SHOE WALKED INTO THE CLEARING wearing the dark glasses, with his ears firmly plugged.

'Good afternoon, Mr Many Coats,' he said casually, even though his mouth had gone dry with fright and his heart banged hard against his chest. 'How is Marigold? I've come to take her home.'

Left Shoe couldn't hear very well with his ears stuffed with cloth, but he saw all of the goannas stop and look at him. Good, he had their attention. Mr Many Coats darted forwards and stared into Left Shoe's dark glasses. The lizard's eyes were like oily black pebbles; like glittering jewels.

But wearing his special glasses, they had no power over Left Shoe. Before the other goannas could do anything, Left Shoe put his plan into action. He told the goannas a joke.

I wish I knew which one it was, but I can never remember jokes. Anyway, by all accounts it was a really pathetic joke, a totally feeble one – the kind of joke your father might tell you to cheer you up, except that it's so unfunny that you can only manage a groan. The goannas, however, thought that this unbelievably poor gag was the most hilarious thing that they had ever heard. They threw back their heads and laughed. Their open mouths revealed nasty forked tongues, which flickered with amusement. Left Shoe found that the earplugs shut out the dangerous sound very nicely. He tried another equally weak joke. The goannas laughed even more heartily. They slapped

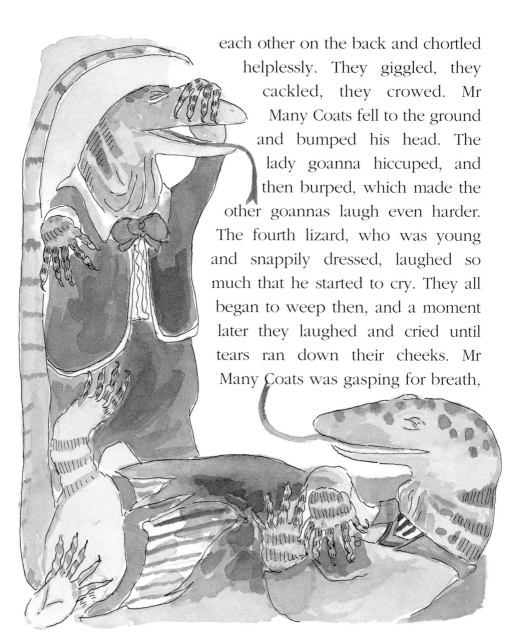

each other on the back and chortled helplessly. They giggled, they cackled, they crowed. Mr Many Coats fell to the ground and bumped his head. The lady goanna hiccuped, and then burped, which made the other goannas laugh even harder. The fourth lizard, who was young and snappily dressed, laughed so much that he started to cry. They all began to weep then, and a moment later they laughed and cried until tears ran down their cheeks. Mr Many Coats was gasping for breath, and he waved his stumpy arms helplessly. It only took one last joke to wear them out altogether. Eventually, when they finally stopped laughing, they were lying breathlessly on the ground. So it was a natural thing for them to fall into an exhausted sleep. Left Shoe signalled to Brass Button and Pink Shell with a little wag of his tail.

The three seadogs removed their earplugs and Left Shoe took off the dark glasses. They crept around the perimeter of the clearing and when they reached the door of the hollow tree jail,

Brass Button and Left Shoe pulled frantically at the rusty latch. It was stuck fast. Pink Shell tried to help but it wouldn't budge. They pushed and pulled until it finally gave way and the door swung open with a groan. They peered into the dank confines of the dark dungeon. It was empty.

Back in the Sandburrow kitchen, Blue Bottle looked through the window at the darkening sky. Already the first stars glittered. She turned to her husband. 'What can be keeping them so long?'

Sea Gem, who had been acting so strangely all day, looked up and smiled. 'Marigold!' she said, and her white face was alight with happiness.

Old Cork looked thoughtful, then rose to his feet. 'Come on, everyone,' he barked, 'grab a lantern!'

Marigold perched on a branch high in the tree, hidden in the shadows. When she looked down, she could see the sleeping goannas. She thought it was safe to remove her earplugs, and

carefully pulled out the scratchy grass. With a jolt of surprise, she saw her brother and cousins below, staring into the dungeon through the open iron door.

'Left Shoe!' called Marigold in the biggest whisper she could manage. 'Look up, silly, I'm here!'

Left Shoe looked up and saw Marigold waving from the high branch. His face lit up with relief.

'Great sea cows, Rig! You nearly gave me a heart attack!'

'Sssh,' warned Brass Button.

'Am I glad to see you!' he added more quietly.

Marigold climbed down to where the others were standing. 'I escaped!' she said, and threw her arms around her brother's waist with a joyful smile. Left Shoe patted her ears shyly.

The goannas snored loudly and muttered in their sleep.

'We've got to get away from here. Follow me,' said Left Shoe.

The children silently gathered their satchels and followed Left Shoe slowly into the clearing. Paw in paw, they sneaked softly past the sleeping lizards, their eyes wide and their hearts thumping. Just as they had almost reached safety, Marigold trod on a stick, which snapped loudly. One of the goannas sat up, blinking his black eyes. It was Mr Many Coats. The pups froze. Each looked to the other, trembling with fright. Slowly, Mr Many Coats stumbled to his feet. When he finally focused on the four terrified pups, his shiny eyes hardened, and he flickered his red tongue hungrily.

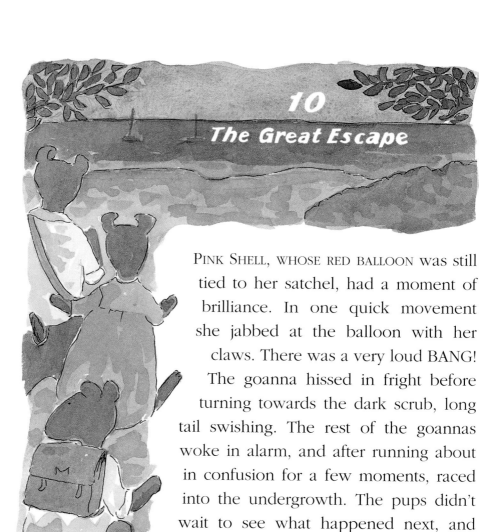

10
The Great Escape

PINK SHELL, WHOSE RED BALLOON was still tied to her satchel, had a moment of brilliance. In one quick movement she jabbed at the balloon with her claws. There was a very loud BANG!

The goanna hissed in fright before turning towards the dark scrub, long tail swishing. The rest of the goannas woke in alarm, and after running about in confusion for a few moments, raced into the undergrowth. The pups didn't wait to see what happened next, and took off towards the beach.

When they reached the water's edge, they kept running. They didn't stop until they were completely breathless, and were forced to slow their pace a little.

Left Shoe kept checking behind them to see if any of the goannas followed. But it was dark now, and it was unlikely that the goannas would have the strength to follow them in the cool night air. Reptiles, you know, need the sun's warmth in order to move around.

'I think we escaped,' panted Left Shoe.

'That was an excellent idea, Pink,' said Brass Button. 'I'd forgotten that goannas hate loud noises.' Then he turned to Marigold. 'Are you all right, Marigold? I mean, that must have been terrible for you, locked in that awful, dark place.'

'Well,' said Marigold, 'it was very scary at first, but then, after a while, it wasn't so bad.'

'Really?' said Left Shoe, impressed. 'But I thought you were afraid of the dark?'

'Well, I was,' replied Marigold thoughtfully, 'but I'm not scared any more.'

The children were quiet for a while. They were suddenly very tired.

'I'm starving,' declared Brass Button.

'Me too,' added Left Shoe.

'The sweets!' remembered Pink Shell. The paper bags were retrieved from her satchel. As the children ate hungrily, Marigold explained how she had found the opening in the top of the hollow tree

jail. After that, Left Shoe told Marigold how they had been hypnotised, and what he had seen in the fortune teller's crystal ball.

'That fortune teller was right,' said Brass Button, when Left Shoe had finished the story. 'But how did she know that Marigold was in danger?'

'She's a seer,' said Left Shoe, 'a special seadog with the power of second sight.'

'Listen!' said Marigold suddenly. They stopped and raised their ears. On the breeze came a soft sound.

'Marigold …'

'It's Father!' said Marigold and Left Shoe at exactly the same time. When the four children reached the glow of the lanterns, their parents embraced them, barking and exclaiming.

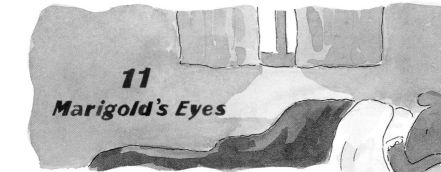

11
Marigold's Eyes

THE NEXT MORNING, Marigold slept very late. Blue Bottle came in with a cup of squink and shook her gently. Marigold sat up sleepily and rubbed her eyes. She wanted to drink the squink, but she was just too tired. She shook her head slowly and lay down again. In moments she had gone back to sleep.

'There, there,' Blue Bottle said softly. 'You sleep. You're safe now.'

Left Shoe hovered in the doorway with his father. He had told Old Cork and Blue Bottle about Marigold's imprisonment in the hollow tree dungeon and their narrow escape from the dreaded goannas. He thought that his father would be angry, but Old Cork had tried to reassure him. Now, seeing Left Shoe's serious face, he put his paw on his son's shoulder.

'It wasn't your fault, Left Shoe. That goanna hypnotised you.'

Left Shoe knew his father was right, but he was still upset that he'd allowed himself to be tricked. His father had told him to stay close to Marigold. He felt he ought to have realised that Mr Many Coats was a goanna.

By the afternoon, Marigold was awake and sitting at the table in the cooking-snug. She had her paper and pencils in front of her, but the page was blank.

'How are you feeling, Marigold?' asked Old Cork.

'Good, thanks,' she replied.

'Are you ready to try on your new glasses?' he inquired gently.

Marigold still wasn't sure she wanted to wear them, but she nodded calmly.

'I'll be back in a moment,' Old Cork said, and he scurried out the door in the direction of his work-snug. When he returned, the other children had gathered to see Marigold's new glasses.

'Marigold,' Old Cork announced, 'close your eyes.' Marigold shut her eyes tight. When she opened them, the blurry feeling disappeared. Perched on the top of her nose was a very smart pair of glasses with wire frames.

'Everything is clear!' she exclaimed. The rest of the children barked their approval.

'Old Cork, you're a marvel!' said Blue Bottle.

Marigold looked around her. It was as if she was seeing everything for the first time. Her family looked perfect in every detail: Shark Tooth's crooked smile, Blue Bottle's round ears, Sea Gem's great blue eyes.

Later, Marigold picked up her paper and pencils and began to sketch. It was easy to draw now that she could see so well. She drew a picture of the leathery gentleman, Mr Many Coats, and when she had finished, she showed it to Old Cork and Blue Bottle.

'That's very good, Marigold,' said Blue Bottle.

Old Cork agreed. The other children came over to see Marigold's picture and they stared at it for a long time.

'Is that what a goanna really looks like?' asked Shark Tooth, her eyes huge.

'Yes,' replied Old Cork. 'You know, Marigold, that's given me an idea. Why don't we send your picture to the *Weekly Bark*? They can print it so that other children can see what a goanna really looks like.'

'Yes,' Left Shoe said slowly, 'maybe we would have realised that Mr Many Coats was a goanna if we'd seen a picture of one. Your drawing looks exactly like him, Rig.'

Marigold said nothing, but smiled shyly. Sea Gem looked up at Marigold and then back to the picture.

'Goanna,' she said, her pale face solemn.

12
The Secret is Revealed

THE NEXT MORNING IT WAS LEFT SHOE'S birthday. Because it was a school day, Old Cork and Blue Bottle told the children that they would have a party that afternoon, with presents and a cake. When school was over, the children arrived at the door, breathless with anticipation.

'Is it time for the party?' asked Shark Tooth.

Old Cork and Blue Bottle stood at the kitchen table. They exchanged mysterious smiles.

'All right then,' said Old Cork, 'are you all ready?'

'Yes!' they cried, barking in excitement.

Left Shoe beamed with pleasure and

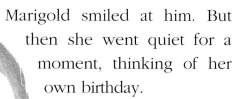

Marigold smiled at him. But then she went quiet for a moment, thinking of her own birthday.

'Now pups!' Old Cork held up a paw to silence the barking children. 'The party is going to be ...' He paused for dramatic effect. 'In the worm-snug!'

There was a gasp of horror.

'The worm-snug!' barked Marigold.

'You must be joking!' Driftwood exclaimed.

'There, there, you'll just have to trust me.' Old Cork turned towards the doorway, chuckling to himself. 'To the worm-snug! Only the brave may follow!'

The children trotted nervously after their father, who held a lantern to light the way. When they reached the little wooden trapdoor leading to the worm-snug, Old Cork turned to them.

'Are you ready, all?' he asked, blowing out the lantern.

He unlatched the worm-snug door and suddenly a yellow circle of light opened up. The pups were amazed. Through the little doorway they could see balloons and decorations along the walls. There was a table set for a party, piled with bowls of sweets, plates of iced cupcakes and a layered cake with pink icing. On top of the cake were two striped, yellow candles. The whole Sandburrow family, with lots of loud barking, descended the ladder into the now fully refurbished worm-snug.

The children were overjoyed. Where there had previously been a terrible, dark hole, there was now a cheerful room flooded with light. Where there had been tree roots and worms, now there was plaster and new paint. Crates of dusty bottles and rubbish had been cleared away and the snug was furnished as a playroom. The shelves displayed their books and toys, and Marigold's pictures hung on the walls. On a table, Left Shoe's pet seahorse, Ajax, swam about in his bowl. But best of all was the skylight. Old Cork had burrowed to the surface, allowing the sunlight to shine down. It was so exciting and perfect in every way that for a moment the children were speechless with delight. Then they remembered that it was a party.

'Happy birthday, Left Shoe!' they cried.

Old Cork grinned broadly. 'Why, it isn't only Left Shoe's birthday, you know.'

'Who else's birthday is it?' asked Shark Tooth, confused.

'Marigold's, of course! It's almost a year since Marigold came to us from the sea, rescued by a very brave seadog.' He ruffled Left Shoe's ears proudly. 'And since we don't know her real birthday, Blue Bottle and I thought that today would be the perfect day for it.' Old Cork looked at the floor for a moment and his voice was low and husky. 'Twins usually share a birthday, don't they?' he said.

Marigold smiled with surprise and delight as she and Left Shoe were ushered to the place of honour at the head of the table. Blue Bottle and Old Cork produced presents, which had been hidden behind a chair. There was a new fishing line for Left Shoe and a glass aquarium containing three hermit crabs.

Marigold received a pretty summer dress embroidered with flowers. But even more wonderful was the second gift. When she unwrapped the parcel tied with ribbon, she blushed with pleasure. It was a bright set of paints in every colour, and a thick book of creamy paper.

'Thank you,' Marigold said, beaming with happiness.

They all sang 'Happy Birthday' in barks, and Marigold and Left Shoe blew out their candles. Thick slices of jam-filled cake were handed around, and all the children listened to the

story of how Old Cork had transformed the dreaded worm-snug into a cheerful play-snug, full of light. The worms, he explained, had been relocated to the wet-snug, a snug never used because it half filled with water when the tide came in.

Sea Gem crawled into Blue Bottle's lap. She laid her head on her paws, but her blue eyes rested quietly on Marigold and Left Shoe. The happy pair laughed together. Their matching glasses made circles around their brown eyes, and sometimes caught the light in little flashes.

'Marigold's home,' said Sea Gem sleepily in her tiny, piping voice.

Marigold looked up at Left Shoe. Feeling her gaze, he turned to her, and then smiled. Even though they weren't born on the same day, they were just the same as proper twins.

Epilogue

The Sandburrow family was very pleased with the transformation of the worm-snug and all of the children spent many happy hours there. Marigold began writing her dictionary in the special book she had been given for her birthday. She drew a picture of a goanna under 'g' for ghastly. After being trapped in the hollow tree dungeon, she wasn't ever afraid of the dark again. She doesn't cry in the night any more, and is never scared if Blue Bottle asks her to fetch something from the dark snugs.

Sea Gem can talk as much as her brothers and sisters now, although she usually watches quietly. Often she plays a harp Old Cork made for her, and sings softly. She still likes the dark, sometimes retreating into its soft blackness to hide. How do I know this? Because it's me, of course, Sea Gem Sandburrow!

THE END

ALMANAC of STRANGE THINGS

Sea Gem's

Goanna A prehistoric lizard that can grow up to three metres long. This cold-blooded reptile has shiny, hypnotic eyes that it uses to subdue its victims, and a few other nasty tricks as well …

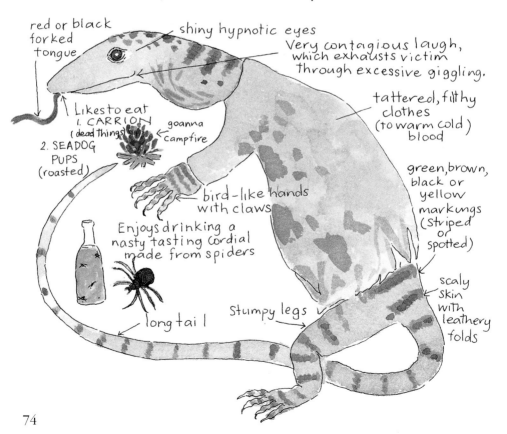

red or black forked tongue

shiny hypnotic eyes

Very contagious laugh, which exhausts victim through excessive giggling.

Likes to eat
1. CARRION (dead things)
2. SEADOG PUPS (roasted)

goanna campfire

tattered, filthy clothes (to warm cold) blood

bird-like hands with claws

Enjoys drinking a nasty tasting cordial made from spiders

green, brown, black or yellow markings (striped or spotted)

scaly skin with leathery folds

long tail

Stumpy legs

Hypnosis A temporary, trance-like state. It can be caused by verbal suggestion (for example, 'Look into my eyes; you are getting sleepy …'), or by staring at a moving object, or looking into the eyes of a hypnotist. The victim of goanna hypnosis goes first into a light trance in which they feel dreamy and light-headed. If they continue to look into the goanna's eyes, they will quickly fall asleep.

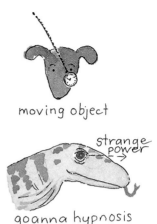

moving object

strange power →

goanna hypnosis

White seadogs White seadogs are very rare. They are always blue-eyed and have to be careful not to get burnt in the hot sun.

sun protection

blue eyes

White seadogs are often gifted with a second sight. A long time ago white seadogs were feared because they were very different from other seadogs. Nowadays the special qualities of white seadogs are revered.

Mirror A smooth surface that reflects a lot of light.

Makes letters appear back to front

Usually made of glass, coated with special paint on the back (paint made from metal).

Light bounces off reflective surface on back.

Right and left sides are reversed.

Cuttlebone

The internal shell or bone of a squid-like creature called a cuttlefish. Seadogs use cuttlebones as money, but they have many other uses as well.

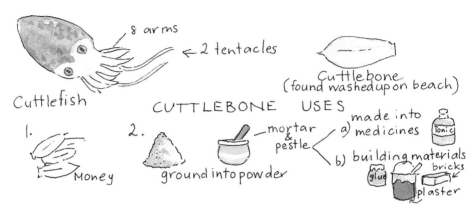

8 arms

← 2 tentacles

Cuttlebone
(found washed up on beach)

Cuttlefish

CUTTLEBONE USES

1. Money

2. ground into powder

— mortar & pestle

a) made into medicines — Tonic

b) building materials — glue, bricks, plaster

Seer

A seer is a seadog who has the power to see events in the future, the past or at a great distance. They are respected for their wisdom. A seer always has a beautiful singing voice. Seers use a special song to communicate with the spirits or the protector of seadogs, the Great Blue Whale.

Great Blue Whale

Seer

Spirits

Fortune-telling

Fortune-telling is seeing future, past or present events using a 'sixth sense'. Fortune tellers sometimes use tools to help them, such as crystal balls, tarot cards, rune stones and tea leaves.

1. Crystal Ball

A sphere made from rock crystal. The seer gazes into it, and it helps to focus the mind. Sometimes pictures appear in the ball.

Seer

2. Tarot Cards

The seer uses these cards to predict the future, or to work out problems.

Tarot cards have colourful pictures. Each has a different meaning.

3. Rune Stones

These are stones with special symbols painted on them. Stones are drawn from a bag. Each symbol has a different meaning.

4. Tea Leaves

Some fortune tellers can see patterns in tea leaves at the bottom of a tea cup. Each pattern has a different meaning.

77

For Stephen, my own Old Cork. Thanks for looking after us.

Thank you to my parents, my family, my friends
and everyone who helped and encouraged me,
especially Nata, Jack M, Robyn S-B, Lisa-Jane, Penny, Brianne and Mrs Geise.

Visit: www.seadogs.com.au
First published in the UK in 2007
by the National Maritime Museum, Greenwich, London, SE10 9NF

www.nmm.ac.uk/publishing

First published 2005 in Macmillan by
Pan Macmillan Australia Pty Limited,
St Martins Tower, 31 Market Street, Sydney

ISBN 978 0 948065 87 3

1

A CIP record for this book is available from the British Library.

Typeset in 13/18 pt Garamond by Seymour Designs
Jacket design by Seymour Designs
Printed in China